This book belongs to

....

Copyright © 2014

make believe ideas ltd

The Wilderness, Berkhamsted, Hertfordshire, HP4 2AZ, UK.
501 Nelson Place, P.O. Box 14100, Nashville, TN 37214-1000, USA.

www.makebelieveideas.com

Written by Tim Bugbird.
Illustrated by Lara Ede.
Designed by Ellie Fahy.

Pippa
the Pumpkin Fairy

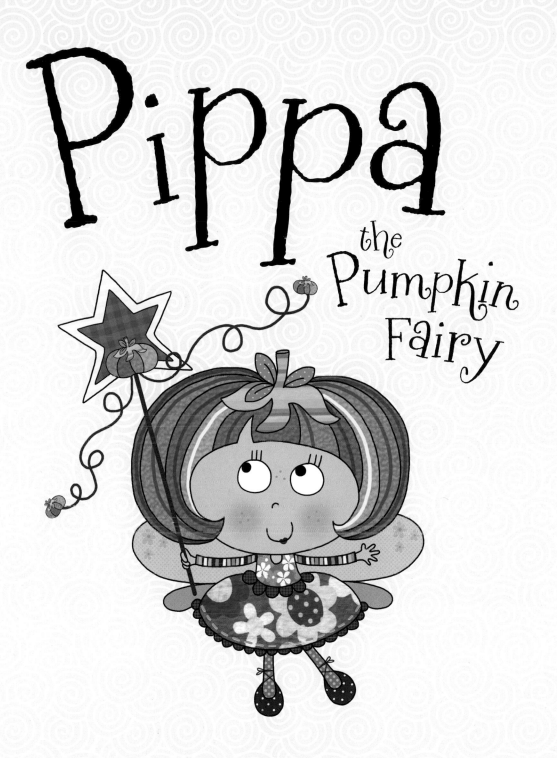

Tim Bugbird · Lara Ede

make
believe
ideas

When Pippa first used her fairy wand,
it was shiny, sparkly, and new.
One whoosh made a pumpkin lantern
and a swoosh made a face with a "BOO"!

The lanterns were made for a party
that came around once a year
when trees were turning golden
and winter was drawing near.

But, one year, Pippa was shocked —

when she waved her wand, she found

all the wrong kind of lanterns

in a row by her feet on the ground!

When Penny and Bea came over to see
how Pippa was getting along,
she panicked and covered the pumpkins.
"Great!" she said. "Nothing's wrong."

"The lanterns are just so BOO-ey,
I had to hide them away.

They're under this cloth so no one can see.

'Til the party, that's where they'll stay!"

"Promise," said Pippa, "you won't tell a soul.
We must not spoil the surprise."

But Penny and Bea **could not** resist
telling a **friend** or **two**.
The news was so **BIG**, and they didn't know
that what **Pippa** said wasn't **true**.

As Penny was talking, Pru overheard
and called Maisie (her very best friend),
who spread the word on Flitter –
Pippa's pumpkins began to trend!

Talk of BOO-tiful pumpkins

soon made the national news

And still Pippa's wand would not work —

she didn't know what to do!

The rumor was getting out of hand.

It was all a terrible mess.

But the longer she left it, the harder it was

for Pippa to try to confess!

The day of the pumpkin party arrived, and the fairies couldn't wait to see just how truly amazing Pippa's lanterns were going to be.

Pippa nervously peeked outside, watched by a TV crew.

"It's time at last!" the presenter announced.

"Pippa, over to you!"

Then, all of the sudden, out of the blue,
lightning cut through the sky.
The fairies looked up as the rain poured down —
they couldn't keep anything dry!

Decorations were soggy, and tables were wet;
the cakes and the snacks were soaked through.
The party was ruined — or so it seemed —
there was nothing the fairies could do!

There was a gasp, then stony silence, followed by laughter and cheers.

The fairies were **applauding** Pippa — she couldn't **believe** her ears!

Pippa's pumpkins weren't BOO-ey at all.
They didn't have "WOO"
or "WAA".

But with their **funny-ha-ha** faces,

they were the **best-ever** lanterns by far!

"We're **sorry** we started rumors," said Bea.

Pippa said, "I'm **sorry**, too.

I got into such a **muddle** —

I should have been **honest** with you."

The **fairies** put on their **ponchos** —
the rain wouldn't spoil their *fun*.

By the light of the laughing lanterns, their party had just begun!

Now, if ever you're in Fairy Land when leaves turn gold from green, you'll find Pippa's pumpkin lanterns the FUNNIEST you've ever seen!